THE
CHRISTMAS TREE RIDE

by Mary Neville

illustrated by Megan Lloyd

Holiday House/New York

For Woody, Kathleen, Christopher, and Connor John
M.N.

For the whole Ruch family,
my "Pennyman" dad, and Tom
M.L.L.

Library of Congress Cataloging-in-Publication Data

Neville, Mary.
The Christmas tree ride / by Mary Neville ; illustrated
by Megan Lloyd. — 1st ed.
p.   cm.
Summary: Two children and their father go to Mr. Pennyman's
tree farm to pick out a Christmas tree and end up making
a new friend.
ISBN 0-8234-0956-2
[1. Christmas trees—Fiction.   2. Christmas—Fiction.]
I. Lloyd, Megan, ill.   II. Title.
PZ7.N464Ch   1992   91-28853   CIP   AC
[E]—dc20

"This Christmas," Dad said,
"will you help me cut the tree?"
He meant Shan and me.
So we got in the car and drove a long way—

out to the country, past the hot dog stands.
"Let's stop," we said. But Dad drove on,
past the drive-ins and the gas stations.
"Take a left," said the filling-station man.

We were skimming along the snow-ice road
till it was *really* country—all frosty and snowy
with silver ribbons floating up from the farm chimneys.
And under the bridges, the streams were ice.

"I don't see any tree farm," Shan said.
"We're getting there," said Dad.

Then we started up, up a hill.
Then down another.
And up, up, up a higher hill made of ice.
I was the one to see the sign.
PENNYMAN'S TREE FARM—ONE MILE.

We found Mr. Pennyman, but his tree farm
was up the road a piece.
"These your kids?" he said, as he climbed in our car
with his ear-flap cap and his ax.
"This road ain't the best. 'Fraid to tackle it?"

Afraid?
Shan and I looked at each other
and Dad.

Then we started on up. That road was steep!
Like a hill made of glass. We got higher and higher.
Far down were the little houses and barns
we'd left behind.

We kept on climbing, but our car went slower
and s l o w e r ,
and s l o w e r .

Over the top!
"Just made it," said Dad.
"The Christmas tree farm!" yelled Shan and I.
There were Christmas trees all over everywhere.
Little baby ones and great big ones
and thin ones and fat ones.

Shan chased me into the trees,
and we gave each other a snow-shower,
standing under a Christmas tree.
It smelled spicy, piney, green.
And it felt snowy, icy, cold.

Mr. Pennyman walked around with his ax.
"Say which one," he said.
"This one," we said.
"No, *this* one."
"No, *that* big, big one over there!"

"How much?" Dad asked.
"It costs a bundle," said Mr. Pennyman.
"Hmmm . . . we'll take the smaller one, then."
CRACK!
Mr. Pennyman hit our tree with a whack.

Dad carried it over his shoulder,
and snow shook down.
Then Dad, Mr. Pennyman, Shan, and I
squeezed back into the car with our own Christmas tree.

We started down the high, high hill.
"Hey!" said Mr. Pennyman.
"You can't back a car down this hill."
But Dad said, "There's no place to turn
without getting stuck." So we started down backward!

Down,
down,
down
the ice hill.
Faster
faster
faster
f
a
s
t
e
r f
a
s
t
e
r!

It was fun!

Shan and I were laughing our heads off.
Dad had his window open so he could see the road,
and he was guiding the car like crazy,
but real calm.

Fence posts whizzed by, the wind whipped in,
cold and nice.
"WHEE-E–E—E!" yelled Shan and I.
"WATCH OUT!" shouted Mr. Pennyman.

We came to a stop.
It was the bottom of the hill,
and we were all right.
Dad looked around and grinned.
Mr. Pennyman took a deep breath.
"Whew," he said.

It took a lot of pulling and hauling
to get our tree up in the living room.
We trimmed it with paper chains,
cranberry necklaces, and shiny glass balls.
Shan and I wrote a secret message
for Mother and Dad on a tiny piece of paper.

We folded it inside a perfect walnut shell,
then tied the walnut halves together with red ribbon,
and hung the walnut deep in the spicy greenness.

Knock, knock! Somebody was at our door.
It was Christmas Eve. We stared, surprised—

there stood Mr. Pennyman holding his ear-flap cap.
He said he was just going by and he thought
he would stop for a minute.
"Come in, come in," said Mother and Dad,
though Shan and I looked at each other.
We were thinking the same thing (we often do).
Didn't Mr. Pennyman have his own house and children
and family to go to on Christmas Eve?

We looked at the Christmas tree, all magic with lights.
Then we sat down and talked.
It turned out Mr. Pennyman did have a house,
but he lived alone. His wife had died, and his
children had grown up and moved away.
"Why don't you come back tomorrow, too," Mother said,
"for Christmas dinner?"

And that's how after the presents on Christmas Day,
there was another knock at the door.
This time we knew who it was, and Shan and I let him in.
He had an ear-flap cap for Shan, and an ear-flap cap for me.
"You'll grow into 'em," he said.
Then we took him to the tree. We'd hung a second
walnut shell. Mr. Pennyman's fingers looked big
as he took his shell apart and looked at the paper inside.
It said MERRY CHRISTMAS
MR. P. !

Christmas dinner was buttery hills
of mashed potatoes and other good things.
We ate a lot, and so did Mr. Pennyman, and Mother and Dad.

Shan and I had decided—
we liked making a new friend
at Christmastime.

And now we can go to Pennyman's Tree Farm
and shake snow down anytime we want—
but 'specially at Christmas.